If our wealth is criminal then let's live with the criminal joy of pirates

If our wealth is criminal then let's live with the criminal joy of pirates

Two stories and an essay
by Jacob Wren

A BOONDOGGLE BOOK
BookThug, 2015

FIRST EDITION

The production of this book was made possible through the generous assistance of the Canada Council for the Arts and the Ontario Arts Council.

LIBRARY AND ARCHIVES CANADA CATALOGUING IN PUBLICATION

Wren, Jacob, author
    If our wealth is criminal then let's live with the criminal joy of pirates : two stories and an essay / Jacob Wren.

ISBN 978-1-77166-184-3 (pbk.)

    I. Title.

PS8595.R454I3 2015   C813'.54   C2015-902624-5

PRINTED IN CANADA

Contents

The Infiltrator

EVERYONE LOVES ME and I love no one. This is a feeling of power. It is what makes the job possible. The job is, in part, to make sure no one ever knows about the job. Like all things in life it might end at any time, but that is not for me to decide. The only evidence of the job is that money is inserted into my account, in wildly differing amounts and at absolutely inexplicable intervals. Otherwise the job is invisible. Every time money is deposited into my account it comes from a different place, a different front. Each of these places, the names of these places, means nothing to me. But I invent a story for each one, in case I am ever asked. Each of these stories must be simple and to the point. If they were complex I would never remember them.

The financial aspects of the job are relatively

straightforward when compared to the rest. When you have money you don't need love. Money makes things happen. But the job requires love or it all goes to hell. Love is connected to power. Or at least that is what I must continue to believe. For much of the time I am alone, reading the exact same books I would read if the job did not exist but I were still placed where I am. There are things I need to know and to know them I must read the books that everyone here reads. I let my mind go blank to enjoy reading these books. The books do not need to be criticized (at least not by me). My fellow activists do not need to be criticized.

When I am doing the job correctly it feels like I don't exist. Something exists but it is not exactly me. Many of the core ideas of the group are based around notions of collectivity and when I feel that I don't exist I also feel that I fit more neatly within this framework. A part of a machine does not go around thinking, Look at me, I am this very specific and important part of the machine. It thinks about the machine, which must function and will function best if all the parts are thinking about the machine. Of course, I am a part of two machines with different goals and different modalities. The machines overlap but the overlap is invisible. And yet at times—in fact, most of the time—I imagine there is only one. One machine pulling in two separate directions, with me as its only common part.

* * * *

The group meets once a month. This is the main gathering, where everyone shares new ideas, talks about what actions we should plan for the future, discusses what was done in the past and how it might have been done better. At these larger gatherings I am always careful to sit as far away as possible from the Irritant. She is the most cynical and also the most suspicious of me. In general, I avoid commenting when she speaks. But when it can't be avoided I take her on earnestly, in as straightforward a manner as possible.

Recently at these meetings it has been suggested there might be an infiltrator among us. This has been the true test of my mettle. How to participate in the conversations about me as if I did not exist? How to participate without giving anything away? I have no tricks or strategy. It is simply a question of speaking genuinely while always leaving out the same key piece of information. I am always careful never to suggest there is no infiltrator, to always leave the possibility open. So far no one has openly suggested it might be me, at least not in my presence, but when they do I must be careful. At that moment it will either end or reach a breaking point past which exposing me will prove impossible.

Along with the main gathering there are also smaller gatherings of two or three members. These smaller meetings are where most of the concrete decisions are made, and present a difficulty in terms of the job. They are where I can have the greatest influence on the day-to-day reality of the group and its actions. But they also contain an intimacy that greatly increases the chance I will be found out, a proximity within which I am far more likely to slip up. As well, I must not attend too many of these smaller meetings because that in itself would be suspicious. It is difficult to ascertain the exact number of smaller meetings I should attend. Attending too few might also raise suspicion, or at least call into question my level of commitment to the group.

Most of the meetings take place in the Girl's apartment. Three weeks ago the Girl and I began sleeping together and now she is completely in love with me. This is another potentially dangerous situation I must monitor carefully. Of course, the Irritant hates the fact that I'm sleeping with the Girl, and I play on this dynamic, hinting at the possibility that what the Irritant has against me is only a kind of non-feminist jealously toward her much younger rival. Since we both know this is not the case I can only apply this strategy sparingly, just a taste of it in the air.

* * * *

When I am doing the job correctly it is almost as if

I am doing nothing. Just the occasional, well-placed suggestion that sends things off along a slightly different path. What amazes me most is how little is required of me as long as I maintain their trust. When I am trusted, when I am loved, my suggestions are simply taken into consideration. If I time these suggestions effectively it is remarkable how quickly they can become the plan for the entire group. But, then again, it is a question of self-discipline. I must be careful, vigilant with myself, in order not to make suggestions too often. If it appears as though I am trying to control things then the game is lost.

At one of the smaller meetings we start talking about corporations. How when you protest against a government it has, at least in theory, a democratic responsibility to take your protest into consideration. But corporations have no such responsibility. They are accountable only to their shareholders. The other guy, the Odd One, comments that, under current conditions, governments in fact are more accountable to the corporations that paid for their campaigns than they are to the citizens who elected them. And there is a kind of consequent logic to this, since the party that spends the most is also the one most likely to win.

I haven't said anything for a while and am asked what I think. I say there must be some way to get at the shareholders directly, since their opinions had the potential to impact the actions of the corporation. I don't know why, in particular, I say this. It is one of the comments I make from time to time that, strictly speaking, could not be said to be part of the job, the logic being that if I only said things the job required my position would appear too imbalanced. I mainly have to say other, more normal things that serve to position me as a committed member of the movement.

So I bring up the idea of directly targeting the shareholders and it is an idea that really catches fire. There follows a continuous stream of suggestions as to what the best way to do so might be. A shareholder makes an investment, the Odd One explains. He or she wants a return on that investment. A profit. This desire for profit is completely disconnected from the daily operations and injustices of the corporation. What we need to do is find ways to connect, within the mind of the shareholder, the investment and the crimes of the corporation. The Girl suggests we could set up a group for concerned shareholders and help them organize. Maybe, she says, there are lots of investors out there who would like to help but feel isolated, don't realize there are others like them.

I decide to let the shareholder brainstorming run its course for a few days before trying to influence it one way or another. If I'm lucky I will find precisely the right spin to get everyone behind the idea of kidnapping a few shareholders. But to be effective my suggestions must come at the right time, and now is definitely not it. It is still only the beginning, when most suggestions will quickly be forgotten, replaced by new suggestions, each idea distorting and confusing the last.

* * * *

That night, after the Girl and I have made love, we lie under the duvet, naked, curled up together, and I feel some tears well up in the corners of my eyes. She notices and wipes them away.

—You're crying.

—Yes.

—Why?

—I don't know. The way the world is going, sometimes it makes me sad.

—Yes. That's why we need to fight.

Only one of us knows I'm lying. Actually, I don't know why I'm crying. Maybe these things have no reason. She has been so kind and tender with me. And I have been completely dishonest. But I'm happy I'm crying and that I can tell her it's because of the current state of the world. It makes me appear sensitive, which within the political logic of the group is important, and it tightens the bond between us, which will serve me well in the future. Now she is crying as well, not too much, just a little bit, like me. I mirror her, wiping away her tears the same way she wiped away mine. She looks at me with genuine concern.

—Do you ever think that what we're doing is pointless?

—Of course. It's only natural to have doubts.

—Then what do you do? To keep going?

—I remind myself it's always better to do something than nothing. If you do nothing then you ensure that nothing will change. If you do something at least you keep open the possibility that something might.

I had read this idea in a book a few weeks ago. I can't remember which one, I'll have to check my notes. When I first read it, it struck me as something that applied to the job as well, only reversed. If I do nothing something might change. And it's only by doing something that things can stay the same. I like these kinds of paradoxes. They keep the job perverse. Without paradox, without perversity, it is impossible to do the job in a convincing way. She is almost asleep now, and the warmth of her body next to mine feels comforting. I wonder what she will think of me if the whole thing blows up. Of course she'd feel betrayed. But in precisely what way would she feel betrayed?

* * * *

Once, when the group was out drinking together, we

came around a corner and the Odd One had completely covered a police car in anti-capitalist posters. We all laughed. It was a genuinely joyous moment. Later, at the main gathering, everyone agreed that he had taken a huge, unnecessary risk. But, the Girl reminded us, we had laughed all night. She couldn't remember the last time she had laughed so much or so hard. And it was a joy we had experienced together, bringing us closer. So wasn't it worth it?

Everyone agreed she had a point but also agreed that the Odd One shouldn't take this as encouragement to "do whatever he wanted whenever the fuck he felt like it." The Odd One just laughed it off and didn't say much in his own defense. It was a joke, was basically all he said. He wanted to live in a world where people could still make jokes and life was fun. Implied was a critique of the group—that we were too serious, too earnest, too much against the miserable things we were against and not enough for the beautiful things we were for. Looking around the room you could tell that this implied critique hit home, that people felt ashamed of their seriousness.

* * * *

This morning, at the café, I see the Irritant and she invites me to join her. All of us go to the café. To read or talk. We've barely started and already she is telling me I can't be trusted. That there's something suspicious about me and the way I interact with the group. She suspects. But I know. And my certainty will always give me the upper hand. I tell her I don't know what to say to reassure her. What does she want me to do?

—Leave.

—But I don't want to leave.

—Sometimes we have to do things we don't want.

—Look, I'm just like you. I believe in collective decision-making. Isn't that one of the things we're fighting for? So if you can convince the others that the best thing would be for me to go, I'll respect the wishes of the group.

She is taken back by my proposal and there is a moment of silence between us, silence filtered through the din of the café. I can see she's pissed off. She doesn't want all the difficulty and hassle of a democratic process. She just wants me out. To do the rounds and convince everyone, one at a time, of my malicious nature might take her a few weeks. I see her formulating her thoughts, trying to dream up the single thing she could say that would be a knockout blow, force me to leave right here and now.

—Who do you work for?

—How do you mean?

—I'm almost sure of it. You're being paid to come here and fuck with us.

—I don't think it serves anyone if we start becoming paranoid.

—There's no "we" here. There's "you" and there's "us."

—I don't understand why you'd say that. It hurts my feelings. I want to do good work. That's why I came here. I believe we can do good work together.

—Why is it so hard to argue with a liar?

—I'm not lying.

—We both know you are.

I wonder what I did, or what it is about me, or about her, that allowed her to catch hold of my tail so quickly. She's more experienced. Maybe she's encountered infiltrators before. I decide to try a direct approach.

—What makes you think that about me?

—It's just . . . obvious. Anyone can see it.

—It's only obvious to you. It's certainly not obvious to the others.

—It will be soon.

I should be unnerved by the café encounter, which ends in a kind of stalemate, but strangely I'm not. I'm sure I can take her. She's respected but she's certainly not loved, often seen as too critical or negative. I'm careful never to be negative at the meetings, always making suggestions positively and with a balanced enthusiasm. And to support other people's suggestions, especially at that moment when the tide is turning and it's clear the suggestion is going to happen anyway.

If love is power, a kind of soft power, it is also true that real power, the kind that makes the job possible, can only operate in secret. When you show your hand you also weaken it. A secret, even when revealed, undermines all certainty, since there might well be more destabilizing secrets to come. I am confident. I will prevail, I know I will prevail, for if I lose their love, if the job crumbles, I have at the very least succeeded in weakening their resolve. I have created suspicions where before there was mainly trust. Then we all know what will occur. It will only take a moment before I completely disappear.

Four Letters from an Ongoing Series

I GET HOME and I check the mail. I dread checking the mail. If there is no mail I feel empty. If there is mail it can only be one of three types: 1) bills I can often not afford to pay, 2) junk mail urging me to purchase something that has almost no connection to my basic desires, 3) letters from far away publishers informing me that they are not going to publish my recently completeld manuscript. Today there is no mail and I feel empty. I unlock my apartment and go inside.

My apartment is full of dust. I clean it and then, a few weeks later, it is completely full of dust again. Every few weeks like clockwork. I clean and, a few weeks later, it is as if the entire apartment has moved backwards in time. When I clean I suspect I don't do a particularly thorough job. But I live alone, am almost never home, so how much cleaning does it actually need? Apparently more than I am currently doing, or at least with greater frequency, with more commitment. Then, thinking along these lines, I feel too much like a man, since cleaning is an unpleasantly gendered activity, one that men, due to considerable social prejudice both in how we are raised and how we are seen or see ourselves, often do with less attention to detail. I hate it when I feel like a man. It is probably even worse when I don't, since those are times I am coasting through territory where my privilege is even more invisible to me than usual.

I am living at a moment in history when people don't use regular mail nearly as often as they used to. When they are far more likely to communicate with each other electronically. It seems likely, in the future but still within my lifetime, that there will be no more mail, or that mail will become something almost exotic, used only on special occasions or by individuals with some slightly nostalgic fetish for handwritten stationary. Will I be one of these stationary-fetish people or will I abandon the mail in the same way I long ago abandoned television and, for the most part, even films? It has been years since I've written anyone a paper letter, but still I check my mailbox every single day with an almost comical sense of dread. The bills pile up on the kitchen table and I pay the ones on the bottom of the pile whenever possible. It is also more than possible for me to pay these bills electronically but I do not, never entirely understanding why I continue to make this particular decision.

I get home and I check the mail. There are no bills, no advertisements. There is however a single letter addressed, via computer-printed label, to my full name. I take it inside, make herbal tea, sit down on a chair at the kitchen table before opening it. It is typed. One page long. I read it slowly and with great trepidation.

Thank you for your generous submission. We have read it, considered it at length, but regret to inform you that we will not be able to publish your manuscript at this time.

We hope the following comments will be constructive, as we have great admiration for your writing, and believe it will eventually find a publishing apparatus that will be able to do it far more justice than we are currently able to.

As we are sure you already well know, these are difficult times for publishing. Your writing is somewhat unusual, yet not so unusual that this sense of difference might be said to be its defining feature. In fact, what precisely might be said to be the defining feature of your writing is somewhat unclear to us. It is political but not overly so. Exploratory but not definitively experimental. Personal yet you in fact reveal fairly little of yourself. Male yet soft.

We could continue, but by this point you might have already caught an inkling of where we are headed. You are in between, fall between the cracks, are neither here nor there. This *in-between* quality is of course the most difficult literary virtue to market. And yet: one might also claim it is your work's main strength and central enigma, the mystery that makes it tick and keeps us reading. Because, we have to admit, once we started your manuscript we were compelled to keep reading until the very end.

Clearly a publisher that is braver than us, with more insight into your work's core strengths, and more savvy in regards to how one might eventually market them, is out there somewhere. We look forward to purchasing a first edition when you and this hypothetical publisher finally meet.

Until then. Wishing you luck.

I put down the letter next to the pile of bills that sits directly beside me. As far as such letters go, this one feels reasonably positive. Useless but positive. If they don't know how to market me than I most certainly don't know how to market myself. Or maybe I do but simply don't want to. Or don't want to quite desperately enough. Or perhaps my desperation is, by this point, sufficient yet blocked by a particularly acute sense of shame. We could also call this shame self-sabotage.

I take a cloth from the shelf, run it under the tap, and halfheartedly drag it over a selection of dusty surfaces. When the first cloth feels too dust-covered to continue, I repeat the activity with a second cloth and then a third. I do so with little order or reason, leaving some surfaces behind, in between clean and dusty, falling through the cracks much – as was just explained to me – like my prose. Then I lie down, read for three hours, a book I find utterly brilliant though later I can't quite remember which one, turn off the bedside light, and lie in the darkness turning the contents of the rejection letter over and over again in my mind. I do this for many hours before eventually falling asleep, not remembering even a single moment of a single dream.

I get home and I check the mail. There is no mail. I unlock the door and head inside. It is well after midnight and I am drunk. I stumble slightly in the kitchen attempting to make tea, and drink it lying in bed, wondering why I drank so much alcohol tonight and if I'm drinking more, or more frequently, than I used to. Will literature last forever or is it practically, already a thing of the past? And how do we even define literature, since without some definition it is barely possible to judge the field's relative health or disrepair. Are my overly refined tastes – predilections and preferences I've spent most of a lifetime overly refining – the most useful criteria or do they pertain only to my personal idiosyncrasies? Would it be better to have something more generalized, a canon most might agree upon, or would this very canon simply be a dampening force, pushing down the lid, creating conventions through consensus both more consensual and more conventional?

One of my overriding goals in life has always been not to become bitter. I'm genuinely not sure if I'm succeeding. Every year I feel a little bit more bitter. And yet there's this voice in my head, repeating almost like a mantra: don't become bitter. Over and over again, off and on throughout the years.

I arrive home and I check the mail. There is one bill, an advertisement for pizza delivery and a letter addressed to me. The address is handwritten, placed neatly in the centre of the envelope. I go inside, place the bill atop the pile of others so much like it, place the ad gently within the recycling bin, fold the letter in half, unopened, since for the moment I have no reason to believe it is not yet another rejection letter, and place it in the breast pocket of my jacket, taking off the jacket and resting it over the back of a kitchen chair. I then make tea. I drink one pot of tea, staring at my jacket as if it were my enemy, facing me down from the back of the chair on the other side of the table. I begin a second pot of tea, a different flavour, knowing I am only procrastinating but telling myself there is no real harm in it. The rejection letter doesn't care if I read it now or in a few hours. I sit drinking tea, don't read or listen to music, the two activities I find myself most often engaged in while at home. I finish the second pot of tea, tell myself this is getting ridiculous, I've waited long enough, reach across the table and into my jacket pocket, tearing the envelope impolitely as I pull it open with my index finger.

Thank you so much for your generous submission. We regret to inform you that we will not be able to publish it at this time. Feel free to submit any future work you manage to complete.

That is it. Two pots of tea worth of dread for only three empty sentences. A form letter. A bit of nothing centred on a blank white page. I place the letter on the table next to the bills, walk to the bathroom and pee. As the urine streams into the toilet I have a depressing thought. That my writing is like this urine, running through me and into the sewer. It comes from my body but is going nowhere, with a single flush no one will ever see it again. Depressing thoughts make me feel stupid, and this negative thought makes me feel stupid with a particular velocity. My book is of course nothing like a stream of urine. What a fucking stupid thought.

I get home and I check the mail. There are two letters addressed to me, an advertisement for someone to shovel my walkway, an advertisement for cheap cable (250 channels) and a telephone bill. I open the door and walk inside, place the bill atop the pile, the ads in the recycling bin. I am still holding the two rejection letters as I start to make tea. The tea is ready and I'm still holding the two rejection letters, standing stock still in the middle of the kitchen. I'm not sure for how long I stay like that, but by the time I read the first letter the entire pot has gone cold and I need to redo it.

Thank you so much for sending us your fine manuscript. We regret to inform you that we will not be able to publish it at this time.

I am only an intern. Therefore, I am not certain to what degree my thoughts and reflections on your work will be of use. However this is the job they're (not really) paying me for and I will therefore do my best to offer your work my honest and focused consideration.

From my perspective, your book is an attempt to bring together two conflicting approaches: a political reflection on the many ways our mainstream Western culture paves over injustices in other parts of the world, injustices it has no small part in creating, and a personal reflection on your own out-of-place, unreflected life (or at the very least the life of a protagonist the reader will have no qualms assuming is little more than a stand in for you). These two streams reflect upon one another yet don't quite connect. This lack of connection might be seen as one of many in your work: between you and the people in your life, between the West and conditions in other parts of the world, between your actual daily life and your desire for emancipatory politics and, possibly with the most (unintentionally?) tragic effects, between the authorial voice and the reader.

The protagonist of your book is marginal. His political views are also, arguably, somewhat marginal. But why should I, as a reader, as someone with a considerably more active and energizing life, particularly care? Resources are violently extracted from poor countries and this very extraction makes my more comfortable lifestyle possible. Reading your manuscript brought this reality, about which I was already hazily aware, towards the forefront of my consciousness. But it didn't make me enjoy my life any less or feel that anything must immediately change.

I am a young man working for free for a smallish, rather prestigious literary press because I can (more or less) afford to. The money (for now) comes from my father, from oil, and the money in my pocket should have most likely remained in the pockets of young people in Iraq or Venezuela. Reading your book makes me think this, but it doesn't particularly make me care. If I'm the enemy then really let me have it. If moral outrage about the state of the world is consuming your life, paralyzing you, taking over your world, then set fire to the reader in an act of revenge. Instead you leave the reader, or this reader at least, indifferent, watching your ineffective life unravel ineffectually. If our wealth is criminal then let's live with the criminal joy of pirates or fight to the death to bring a sliver more of justice into being. Not the passive slither forward you are attempting to pass off as literature.

I realize all of this is easier said than done. And I am only an intern here, what do I know. Feel free to send us any future work. By that time someone else will be doing my (thankless) job and I will hopefully be a little further up the ranks.

I put down the first letter and stare at the still unopened envelope of the second. Right now, somewhere in the world, probably somewhere far away but perhaps also somewhere close, someone is being bombed and someone else is being tortured. But not me. I have finished the pot of tea and begin to make a second (actually a third if we include the one I let grow cold). I have a moment of wanting to kill that intern and then another moment of feeling thankful he was so honest and provocative. There is so little honesty in the world.

I haven't cleaned my apartment in weeks, or maybe months. And silently, as if in a trance, as if I barely even know what I'm doing, I fold the second letter in half, place it in my jacket pocket and begin. I fill a bucket with almost-boiling soapy water and start wiping down every surface I can find. I wash the walls and mop the floors. Scour the bathtub and the inside of the toilet. I carefully take the dust from the top of every single book in my library, wash the windows and clean out the fridge. By the time I'm finished it is almost 3 a.m. I wonder if I should read the second letter now or wait until morning. Would it actually be possible for me to fall asleep not knowing what it says? Am I exhausted enough? I shower, standing under the plentiful hot water like a corpse, wondering how many of these letters I will continue to collect.

Lying in bed, staring at the ceiling, I realize there is no way I'm getting any sleep tonight. I walk to the kitchen to get the second letter, quickly tearing it open.

We kindly regret to inform you we will not be accepting your manuscript for publication at this time. Here are some thoughts on the matter:

Writers always seem to think their lives are so interesting. Yours, like most writers, is not. In your work you almost seem to know this, and therefore fill the void with reflections on politics and the world. These reflections are somewhat more intriguing. But we are not a political press and, in general, radical politics is a hard sell. We are in the business of selling books, quality literary books, and have little interest in either promoting your self-pity or in attempting to change the world.

I am an educated man, and know as much about politics as many educated men. However, I am no expert and will not comment further on the political scope of your writings, except to say you might well be better off writing pamphlets and handing them out on street corners. What I am, unfortunately, is an expert on the self-pity of unpublished literary writers. I have come to this expertise, of course, through my job reading endless slush piles of words that, at times, seem to me to be little more than expressions of this self-same, middle-class guilt and self-pity.

I will now say to you what I have so often wanted to say to so many of these writers. More commonly I restrain myself in the name of professionalism, but while reading your manuscript something in me snapped. I hope, once the initial sting has receded, you will be able to take this advice. God knows you need it more than most.

So here is goes: get out there and fucking do something with your life, it's not too late. Have love affairs, protest the government and go to jail for it, get into fights, run for office, set fire to a police car or to an oil well, go to

other countries and feed the poor, kill someone who deserves to die, save someone's life,
take too many drugs, start a business or a band
or a drug smuggling ring. For god sakes, do
something, anything, so you'll have something
to write about other than your own pathetic
life and your own pathetic reflections on how
obviously unfair the world is.

Or, if all that seems too much, at least make
something up. Write science fiction, invent
other worlds or other species. If you don't have
any adventures of your own then holy fuck
just make some up. Don't just stare at the mirror bemoaning your tepid fate, use your imagi-
nation to send yourself towards some better, or
at least more interesting, world.

I will not apologize for my little rant because I
honestly think you need it, because I want you
to take it square in the face. You have potential but you're wasting it on mundane, writerly
self-pity. Wasted potential is heartbreaking.
Take this letter to heart and actually change
your life.

It was strange to get those two, both rather critical
letters at the same time. I lie in bed filled with doubts

of every kind. And yet, if I'm honest with myself, I strangely don't doubt my work all that much. I have to write the books I have to write. If every single publisher in the world thinks they're shit than so be it. Of course it feels bad now but I'm sure I've seen worse and perhaps there is even worse to come. Right now, somewhere in the world, someone is being tortured and someone else is being bombed. How much do a few pages of critical words directed at me really hurt when stacked up against even a sliver of the horrors possible in the world? I'm going to keep writing books, I try to tell myself, not sure if I'm still completely awake or if I'm already drifting off to sleep. And if not, maybe it's still not too late to find some other thing to do with my life.

The next morning, the mood from the previous night continues but in a slightly different key. Since I'm arrogant, I tell myself, or at least confident – I know that my manuscript is good and that, someday, instead of this trickle of rejection letters, my work will instead be met with any number of appreciative offers, perhaps not this current book but some future, as yet unwritten one. In the long run I will be read. Whether this happens while I'm still alive, or long after, remains difficult to say. It might happen tomorrow or perhaps in a hundred years. However, if this flood of success were to miraculously occur tomorrow, if I were then easily able to pay my few bills and no longer had to read these endless letters of rejection, I also fear it would make little difference to my mood or to my life. My life might improve, might even improve considerably, but I suspect I would feel more or less the same. I get home and I check the mail. Today the mailbox is empty, there is nothing. I unlock my apartment and go inside.

Like a Priest Who Has Lost Faith

Notes on art, meaning, emptiness and spirituality

I.

IS IT TRUE THAT TODAY, in casual conversation, art-
ists often speak about wanting to have a career, but
rarely speak about wanting to make something meaningful? Or is this casual observation only my cyni-
cism rising to the surface? In the most general sense,
the hope that art can be meaningful in people's lives
brings it very close to the spiritual, and this might be
one of the many reasons the topic is often avoided. If
I say I want a career (which, of course, I do as much as
any artist) I might come across as ambitious, but there
is also something practical and down-to-earth in my
pronouncement. If I say I want to make something
meaningful it is a higher style of arrogance, more old
fashioned, less critical and therefore less contempo-

rary. The desire to make something meaningful brings along with it a thousand small distastes and taboos.

When you like (or love) a particular work of art, and happen to meet someone else who feels the same way, it creates a sense of possibility: for connection, for the potential that shared values might exist, that these values might be articulated (and questioned) in relation to a shared experience. This is the agency of the work of art, to draw you towards itself and open up peculiar opportunities for connection amongst disparate individuals. This possibility for unexpected connection is, for me, the edge along which art draws closest to the spiritual. Or to put it another way, a sense of ongoing connection, with friends or strangers, in relation to an object or idea outside ourselves, is the closest my thought gets to spirituality.

Let me attempt a rough definition: the spiritual is a sense that there exists something larger than us, larger than us as individuals and larger than us as humanity. There is not just us and what we see in front of us, there is also something else, and it is through this something else we are able to experience ongoing connections between us. This definition is so rough that, using it, we could easily say that fascism is a form of (debased) spirituality. And of course it is. If we don't get the real thing, if we are not allowed a genuine sense that the gods or spirits exist, that there is something otherworldly to believe in, we will search for every kind of possible substitute.

(I used fascism as my first example, but fear this was only empty provocation. Of course, using my rough definition, a more obvious example would be to say that a felt connection to the natural world – with plants, animals and ecosystems – is extremely spiritual. Many do, and at this point in our disastrous ecological freefall, it is hard to argue.)

Like many of us, I am in crisis (with one possible difference being that I have a compulsion to announce my sense of crisis as often as possible). I am in crisis about art and also about everything else. There are many ways I have attempted to describe this crisis, but the one I use most often is as follows: I feel like a priest who has lost faith in God, but continues to give a weekly sermon anyway. This description has something to do with making performances, with the feelings engendered by getting up in front of a room full of people, people who are there to watch you, and performing something for them (or for yourself yet in front of them). About the anxiety that what one is doing may, or may not, be meaningful to many of those present. The performance situation itself suggests a certain potential for connection among a room full of strangers, but this connection is bound to (at least partly) fail, because when the performance is over the connection is severed, is relegated to memory.

If the congregation believes in God, but the priest giving the sermon does not, there is an unbridgeable chasm of intention between what is being said and how it is perceived. If the priest believes in God, but the congregation does not, then one might wonder why they even bother to attend in the first place. Yet even if everyone in the room believes like crazy, there is always a paradox at work in the heart of the experience, since it is the belief itself, the faith and the fact that it is shared, that generates the sense of connection. And, vice versa, the connection that generates a sense of faith. A classic feedback loop. We feel connected to the people who surround us because we all believe in the same thing, and our belief is continually reinforced by our sense of feeling connected to each other.

All of this has very little to do with my actual experiences of watching contemporary performance or looking at contemporary art. I am much too secular, too isolated, for such examples to take on a life of their own. Nonetheless they are analogies that feel potent to me, that speak to a certain lack. When I walk into a contemporary art exhibition what is it exactly that I am supposed to believe in? How many of these beliefs am I expected to bring with me prior to my experience of looking at the work, and what aspects of these beliefs, these preconceptions, are necessary for me to be able to experience it?

I am astonished how empty I often feel after watching a performance or viewing an exhibition. I always wonder how many others feel this way, why more people I know don't speak of their experiences of art in these terms? It is as if everyone involved in art is simultaneously expected to be a cheerleader for the cause, to keep reciting the sermon every Sunday whether they feel it or not. You are allowed to say you want a career, but you are not allowed to say you want more meaningful art experiences. All of this, of course, makes me wonder what I would need from art in order to feel less empty.

2.

In his 1991 book *We Have Never Been Modern,*[1] Bruno Latour argues that the scientific separation between nature and human affairs that marked the onslaught of modernity – the revolution that severed the modern from the premodern world – in fact never occurred. Instead of clearly dividing the natural world from the human one, Latour posits that modernity formed around a series of crafty double games, playing nature against society and vice versa, utilizing critique of both past and present to generate complicated hybrids and paradoxes that become impossible to circumvent. For example, on the one hand modernity says "nature is not our construction, it is transcendent and surpasses us infinitely," and "society is our free construction, it is immanent to our action." But, at the same time, it also says "nature is our artificial construction in the laboratory; it is immanent," and "society is not our construction, it is transcendent and surpasses us infinitely." While these two positions might, at times, be debated by individuals on opposite sides of a given argument, when taken in their entirety they form a worldview that is utterly inconsistent, and can utilize it's own inconsistencies as a pretext to take power and exploit the natural world. While the modern might claim that primitives were full of irrational beliefs, Latour demonstrates that modern beliefs are equally (or even more) irrational, that they are matters of faith.

I recently became interested in Latour while reading a interview with him in *Animism I*, the first of two catalogues from a touring exhibition curated by the artist Anselm Franke. Two short sentences in an interview with Latour struck me with particular force: "What is the action of the gene? What does it do and where does it come from?" These questions occurred in the

40

midst of a discussion on animism, when Latour decides to speak of animism not in terms of belief systems of previous cultures, but simply as the possibility that objects, and by extension the natural world, have agency. He imagines confronting a hypothetical critic of Franke's exhibition:

> Now, you are anti-animist. Does that mean there is no agency in the world? At all? Your interlocutor would say, yes, of course there is agency. Atoms have agency, cells have agency, stars have agency, psyches have agency; and then you begin to look at the specificity and the specification of all these agencies, and you realize that you begin to jump from one field to the other. . . . So we begin to have a whole series of transports, of agencies from one domain to the other. Biology would be full of it. The whole question of agencies in biology is the gene. What is the action of the gene? What does it do and where does it come from?[2]

I believe this question struck me so forcefully because it took me back to the anger I felt, in the early nineties, reading *The Selfish Gene* by Richard Dawkins. (The opening sentences of this text might well be subtitled 'the selfish artist.') The feeling I had that, in the wrong hands, evolution was little more than a tepid creation myth: once upon a time there were genes that wanted to preserve themselves and these genes evolved and evolved until eventually they became people. The misguided anthropomorphism with which Dawkins speaks of these genes infuriated me, as did his misplaced anger towards religion, which in fact he only wants to replace with his own theory, a theory that is considerably less complex and resonant. It seemed to me that if Western modernity is going to have a creation myth, the very least we could do is come up with something helpful, something that offers solace, something that makes life better instead of worse. And then this well-known quote from Darwin: "It is not the strongest of the species that survives, nor the most intelligent that survives. It is the one that is the most adaptable to change."

Unfortunately, I have not seen Franke's exhibition. I have only read the catalogue, which begins:

> For most people who are still familiar with the term "animism" and hear it in the context of an exhibition, the word may bring to mind images of fetishes, totems, representations of a spirit-populated nature, tribal art, pre-modern rituals and savagery. These images have forever left their imprint on the term. The expectations they trigger, however, are not what this project

concerns. Animism doesn't exhibit or discuss artifacts or cultural practices considered animist. Instead, it uses the term and its baggage as an optical device, a mirror in which the particular way modernity conceptualizes, implements, and transgresses boundaries can come into view.[3]

The exhibition, inspired by Latour, desires to examine animism in order to question whether modernity's claims of having broken with the past are accurate. From the images in the catalogue, all of which are intriguing, I believe it stages this inquiry as a strong contemporary art exhibition, with photographs, videos, installations, historical materials, wall texts, etc. The exhibition clearly doesn't want to be animist, it only wishes to make use of the topic in order to ask extremely pertinent questions. (Questions I am clearly fascinated by.)

There is something ironic in using critique and questioning, the modern strategies *par excellence*, in order to undermine the assumptions of modernity. Latour is clear that there is no point in critiquing modernity – since modernity continually thrives on critique in order to reinvent itself, creating new hybrids and paradoxes in the process – and instead suggests that we must go somewhere else, find another way of looking at the world, another way of understanding our relation to the past. Strategies used by the Animism exhibition suggest there would be no way for an exhibition today to embody an animist worldview, such a thing could only take place if the viewers themselves were believers. However, it is also true that we simply don't know, since no attempt is made to imagine what kind of exhibition might embody a spirit of animism today. In its refusal to struggle with the possibility that works of art do have a life of their own – in that we, at times, believe in them, and that this belief can actually make us act, lead us do or think in ways we would have never otherwise considered – I suspect an opportunity is missed, a challenge that may well be taken up by some future project.

I wonder if the framework in which most contemporary art attempts to generate meaning is analogous to the 'never been modern' framework that Latour criticizes. Art is a world that separates, continuously playing the divisions against one another in ways that are often contradictory: good art against bad, art against everything else, political art against commerce, etc. The gallery is a place for art, but it is also a way of removing art from the rest of life. In my earlier analogy of the priest who has lost faith, I move back in time towards Christianity (a faith I have no personal experience with) but perhaps I don't go back far enough. I have not read nearly enough anthropology to know about previous cultures, previous ways of life, but following Latour's lead I would like to imagine an art, society and worldview that is considerably less divided. (Latour calls this position 'amodern.') If nature is alive then it can, of course, speak to us. And if art is anything, it must have some life of it's own, but a life far more integrated with our daily impulses and actions. These are ideals I have not taken even the smallest step towards. Nonetheless, I wonder about such matters constantly.

Richard Sennett writes: "Ritual's role in all human cultures is to relieve and resolve anxiety, by turning people outward in shared, symbolic acts; modern society has weakened those ritual ties. Secular rituals, particularly rituals whose point is co-operation itself, have proved too feeble to provide that support."[4] Going to galleries and performances is a kind of ritual, as is making any kind of art. But they are weak rituals indeed, full of bad faith, ego and careerist intentions. Why can't we create works of art, and philosophies, that actually help us live our lives? Why does this question feel so naive and ridiculous to me? From the beginning of time utopians of every stripe have been searching for a less divided world, and there is certainly no reason to stop searching today.

Notes

1. Bruno Latour, *We Have Never Been Modern*, trans. Catherine Porter (Cambridge: Harvard UP, 1993).

2. Anselm Franke, "Angels without Wings: A conversation between Bruno Latour and Anselm Franke," *Animism,* ed. Anselm Franke (Berlin: Sternberg Press; Antwerp: Extra City; Antwerp: Museum of Contemporary Art, 2010), 1:86–96.

3. Anselm Franke, "Much Trouble in the Transportation of Souls, or: The Sudden Disorganization of Boundaries," *Animism,* 1:11–53.

4. Richard Sennett, "All together now: Montaigne and the art of co-operation," *Guardian*, February 10, 2012.

Acknowledgments

'The Infiltrator' was originally published in *Maisonneuve*.

'Four Letters from an Ongoing Series' was originally published in *Joyland*.

'Like a Priest Who Has Lost Faith' was originally published in *Etc.*

Colophon

Produced in celebration of Authors for Indies Day, 2 May, 2015. Support your local independent bookseller.

Edited and designed by Malcolm Sutton
Typeset in Portrait Text

BOOK
PRODUCTION
WAR ECONOMY
STANDARD

Shop online at www.bookthug.ca